Cataloguing data available from Library and Archives Canada
ISBN 978-0-9918588-3-5

Text by Michael Mayes
Jacket and text design by Paul Roelofs
Illustrations by Rory O'Sullivan

Printed and bound in China by C&C Offset Printing Co., Ltd.
Distributed in the U.S. by Publishers Group West

Knowledge Network
Burnaby BC Canada
www.knowledge.ca

Figure 1 Publishing
Vancouver BC Canada
www.figure1pub.com

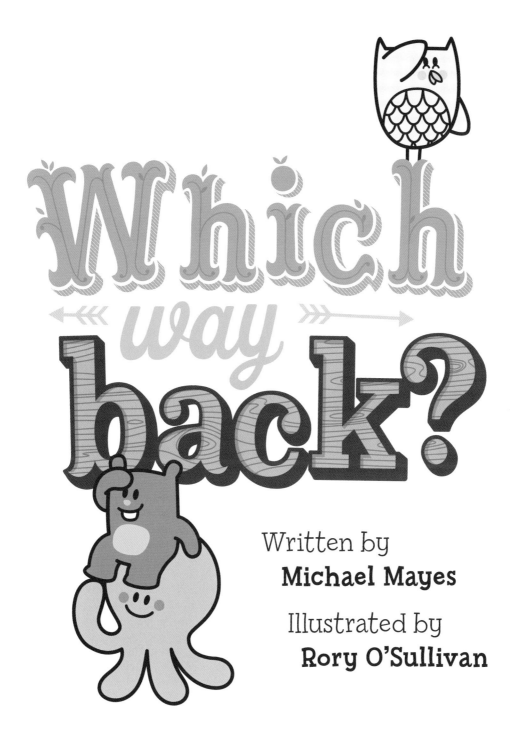

Which way back?

Written by

Michael Mayes

Illustrated by

Rory O'Sullivan

Knowledge:kids

FIGURE 1 PUBLISHING

Vancouver

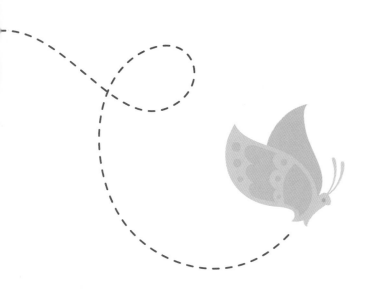

To childhood adventures
that last a lifetime in our memory

One sunny afternoon Luna, Chip and Inkie
were skipping rocks across Eagle Lake.

Luna was looking for a flat rock to skip
and saw a butterfly on a blade of grass.
"Wow! That's the biggest butterfly I've
ever seen!" Luna said.
Chip and Inkie ran over
to see it too.

Startled, the butterfly flew up over their heads and fluttered off into the forest.

"Let's follow it!"

Chip shouted, and he ran into the forest, chasing after the butterfly.

Luna and Inkie ran after Chip, jumping over logs and ducking under branches trying to catch up.

"Wait for us!"

Inkie yelled. But Chip was fast. He was getting farther and farther ahead.

When they finally
caught up with Chip,
he was standing on a
rock by a creek, looking
into the sky.

"Chip! We found you!" Luna said.

"Found me?" Chip said. "I wasn't even lost! But I lost the butterfly. Oh well." Chip shrugged and hopped down from the rock.

"I think we'd better get back to Eagle Lake," Luna said.

They had explored lots of places near Eagle Lake,
but they had never been this far from home before.
They had never seen this part of the forest.

"Isn't this Eagle Creek?" Chip asked.
"I don't think so," Inkie said.
"Let's just go back the way we came," Luna suggested.
Luna, Chip and Inkie looked around.

They couldn't tell which way was back!

**Suddenly, they were
all very worried.**

Chip was worried they wouldn't
make it home for dinner.

Inkie was worried they wouldn't make it home before dark.

Luna was worried they
wouldn't make it home...at all!

They worried for a while.

They argued for a while.

They thought for a while.

And then, Luna had an idea.

She flew up as high as she could to see
what she could see and reported back.

"From up there, I saw two creeks!" she said. "Both creeks in the forest run from Eagle Lake down to the ocean," Luna explained.

"So, if we go upstream, we'll get back home!"

Chip frowned and kicked a rock.

"What's wrong, Chip?" Inkie asked.
"Luna knows the way back."

"Upstream!"

Chip sighed. "I thought I could
build us a raft or something, but that
would only get us downstream!"

Then Inkie had an idea out of the clear
blue sky. Maybe because the sky above
them was getting darker and Inkie really,
really wanted to get home soon.

She drew her plan in the dirt to show Luna and Chip.

"That plan will totally work!" Chip shouted,

and he ran back into the woods.
Chip came out with a bunch of fallen
trees and started chopping them
into pieces with his teeth.

With logs and twigs and leafy things they found in the forest, Chip, Luna and Inkie built a raft strong enough to carry them on the creek.

They pushed it into the water and hopped on.

It worked!

Inkie swung her legs off the raft into the water and spun them as fast as she could. The raft zoomed upstream like a motorboat.

"Wooooo!"

Luna shouted as they splashed up the creek.

Chip used his tail to steer while
Inkie kicked hard with six legs and held
on tight with two. Luna looked
for Eagle Lake up ahead.

Then, just as the sun set behind the treetops
Luna, Chip and Inkie floated onto Eagle Lake.

They were so happy to be home, they
almost forgot how worried they had been
and how lost they had felt.

But they never forgot how lucky they
were to have friends like each other.

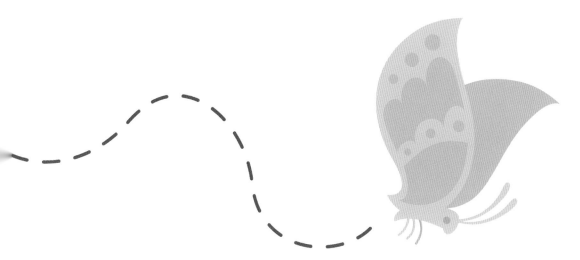

The End

More about Knowledge Kids

British Columbia's Knowledge Network is the trusted public broadcaster behind Knowledge Kids. Hosted by Luna, Chip and Inkie, it offers a commercial-free world where stories come to life and adventures await around every corner. **Which Way Back?** is the first picture book featuring the energetic trio who make their home in British Columbia's wilderness.

We hope you enjoy the story.
For more go to **knowledgekids.ca**

Proceeds from the sale of this book support Knowledge Network's mission to offer media that spark a child's imagination and love of learning.

Meet Luna

Luna is a fairly quiet owl. Usually, it's because she's thinking. She loves to learn and notices lots of fascinating things around her. She's not afraid to ask questions and tries to figure things out for herself, if she can. Sometimes Luna worries a bit too much, but her friends always help her relax and have fun. When Chip and Inkie aren't around, Luna reads and she writes poetry and songs. She also likes to collect neat objects she finds wherever she goes. "For inspiration!" she says.

Meet Chip

Chip is an extremely busy beaver. He likes to build stuff, explore new places and jump into pretty much anything he can. He often does things before thinking them through and accidentally ends up in more trouble than anyone. But Chip always learns from his mistakes along the way. With his positive attitude, kind heart and big toothy smile, he's always back in everyone's good books before too long. Chip likes to breakdance, belly-flop and try any kind of new stunt, especially if it involves his tail.

Meet Inkie

Inkie is one creative octopus. She paints, acts, plays the guitar and knows dozens of ways to make her friends laugh. Inkie loves entertaining everyone and making new friends. She knows English, Oceanic and Animal Sign Language, so she can communicate with almost anyone, anywhere. She's also a very good listener and uses her creativity to help solve problems. Inkie doesn't like it too much when she's not good at something, but her friends always make her feel great for who she is, no matter what.